For my cousin, Michelle, who lovingly shapes my world each day

and selflessly supports at-risk youth, helping them on their way —SBK

To my father, who taught me drawing just sitting next to me —EO

Text copyright © 2016 by Susan B. Katz
Illustrations copyright © 2016 by Eiko Ojala

All rights reserved. Published by Orchard Books, an imprint of Scholastic Inc., *Publishers since 1920.* ORCHARD BOOKS and design are registered trademarks of Watts Publishing Group, Ltd., used under license. SCHOLASTIC and associated logos are trademarks and/or registered trademarks of Scholastic Inc.

The publisher does not have any control over and does not assume any responsibility for author or third-party websites or their content.

Library of Congress Cataloging-in-Publication Data Available

ISBN 978-0-545-74100-2

10 9 8 7 6 5 4 3 2 1   16 17 18 19 20

Printed in Malaysia   108
First edition, January 2016

The display type was hand-lettered by the illustrator.
The text was set in Neutra Text Demi.
The illustrations were rendered in pencil on paper
and recreated digitally.
Book design by Patti Ann Harris

ALL YEAR ROUND

words by
Susan B. Katz

pictures by
Eiko Ojala

Orchard Books • New York
An Imprint of Scholastic Inc.

A world of shapes,

TWELVE MONTHS

abound,
from four-cornered square,
to circle, round.

CIRCLE

round,
ready to roll.
Add two sticks,
a carrot, and coal.

January

Cut out a

HEART

for a special friend.
Write a message,
lick, stamp, send.

February

An **OVAL** egg
starts to crack.
Out comes a duckling.
Quack! Quack!
Quack!

March

April

A HALF CIRCLE,

don't let go.
Showers, sunshine,
a real rainbow!

A simple

SQUARE,

colorful flowers,
brought to you
by springtime
showers.

May

A sporty

DIAMOND,

player at bat.
Bases loaded,
tilt your hat.

June

A regular

RECTANGLE

can be cool.
For a summer swim,
dive into
a pool.

July

August

This brown **CONE** will be quite yummy.
With a double scoop,
it'll melt in your tummy.

A red **OCTAGON,**
follow the rule,
when crossing the street,
walking to school.

September

Pick your
SPHERE

when it's done growing.
Carve it out.
Look, it's glowing!

October

November

TRIANGLE

treats,
pumpkin, peach.
Want some pie?
Excuse my reach!

December

A rink of children learning to skate. Graceful couples,

A FIGURE EIGHT.

Each shape has a match,

from January to December.

What's your favorite pair?

How many can you remember?